The Torchbearer

by Susan Blackaby
illustrated by Len Epstein

PiCTURE WiNDOW BOOKS
Minneapolis, Minnesota

Editor: Shelly Lyons
Designer: Abbey Fitzgerald
Page Production: Michelle Biedscheid
Art Director: Nathan Gassman
Associate Managing Editor: Christianne Jones
The illustrations in this book were created digitally.

Content Adviser: Brian S. Hook,
Associate Professor, Department of Classics
University of North Carolina Asheville

Picture Window Books
5115 Excelsior Boulevard
Suite 232
Minneapolis, MN 55416
877-845-8392
www.picturewindowbooks.com

Printed in the United States of America.

All books published by Picture Window Books
are manufactured with paper containing at least
10 percent post-consumer waste.

Library of Congress Cataloging-in-Publication Data
Blackaby, Susan.
The torchbearer / by Susan Blackaby ; illustrated by Len Epstein.
p. cm. — (Read-it! chapter books. Historical tales)
ISBN 978-1-4048-4063-8 (library binding)
[1. Elephants—Fiction. 2. Rome—History—Republic,
265-30 B.C.—Fiction.] I. Epstein, Len, ill. II. Title.
PZ7.B5318Tor 2008
[Fic]—dc22   2007032897

Table of Contents

Words to Know

cargo—goods carried by a ship, airplane, or truck

harbor—a sheltered place along a coast where ships and boats anchor

Julius Caesar—one of ancient Rome's greatest leaders; he helped build a huge Roman Empire

navigator—the person on a boat who is in charge of determining or steering a course

port—a place where ships and boats dock

Roman Empire—ancient Rome's political territory; it was at its strongest point about 2,000 years ago

Roman Numerals

Roman Numeral	Number
I	1
II	2
III	3
IV	4
V	5

Roman Numeral	Number
VI	6
VII	7
VIII	8
IX	9
X	10

Marcus and Camilla had been waiting for days for their father's ship, the *Rising Star,* to arrive. It was due to sail into port any day. They played on the beach, sometimes stopping to scan the water for the ship. They wanted to meet their father when his ship docked.

5

As Marcus watched the horizon, a speck appeared. He kept his eye on it. It grew bigger as it moved toward shore. He pointed and asked, "Is that it?"

Camilla followed his gaze until she saw the ship.

Her eyes were sharper than his. She claimed that she could spot their father standing at the ship's wheel. Marcus did not think she could. Yet she always knew the *Rising Star*, even when it was far out to sea.

Camilla jumped up. "Yes!" she yelled. "It is Father!"

The children turned and raced up the beach. Their feet kicked up clouds of sand behind them. They came to the edge of the city and ran up to the first row of apartments. Their mother waved from the balcony.

"The *Rising Star* is coming into port!" yelled Marcus.

"So I see," said Mother. "You kids go and meet your father. I will start fixing the meal. Camilla, come home soon. You can help me."

"All right," said Camilla.

"Marcus, do not make a pest of yourself if you are not needed," said Mother.

The kids hurried down to the docks.

Marcus loved living near the sea. During the summer months, cargo ships like the *Rising Star* sailed into the harbor every day. They carried gold, silver, and copper. They carried olive oil and grain. They carried pottery, wool, and spices.

Of all the cargo that came in, Marcus liked the animals best. Sometimes they arrived from Africa. Often they came from faraway ports to the east. Crates and cages lined the docks. Birds fluffed their bright feathers. Leopards paced. Giraffes stretched their long necks. Elephants raised their trunks like arms.

Seeing the animals close-up amazed Marcus. He got a good look while they waited to be loaded onto barges and boats. The smaller ships transported the animals to Rome.

Once the animals got there, they competed in games and contests, marched in parades and festivals, and amused visitors and guests.

When Marcus and Camilla got to the dock, they pushed past the crew to get on the ship. They met their father on deck. He hugged them.

"Did you bring me an elephant, Father?" Marcus asked.

"Not this time," Father said with a wink.

That evening, the family ate together. Father told them about the things he had seen. As always, the kids had many questions.

"How was the trip?" Camilla asked.

"Rough," said Father. "It is almost winter. Soon it will be time for crossing the sea to stop."

Father spoke too soon.

Chapter II

Late Crossing

Usually shipping slowed down in the fall and stopped for the winter. This year, however, the sea did not close. There was a late stretch of sunny, fair weather. The ships kept coming and going. It was nearing the end of October, but the port stayed busy.

Father was the navigator on the *Rising Star*, and he decided to make two more quick trips to Carthage.

While Father was gone, the men on the dock put Marcus to work. He unloaded sacks and crates from dawn to sunset.

When Father returned again, Marcus asked,
"Did you bring me an elephant?"

Father answered, "Not this time."

In the middle of November, Marcus and
Camilla found Father packing to leave.

"We are making one last run today," said Father.

"What will you be carrying?" Camilla asked.

"We will take over a load of pottery. We will bring back a load of grain," he answered.

Marcus knew that if the weather was good, it would be a 10-day trip. If the weather was bad, it could take 15 days or more.

"Isn't it getting risky to cross?" Marcus asked. "If bad weather arrives, it will be the end of November before you can get back. By then, the winds will make it difficult to cross."

"Marcus is right," said Camilla.

"Don't worry," said Father. "I have clear skies and fair winds. We will make it to Africa in three days. One day to unload and load up again, and we will be on our way home. I will see you in no time!"

A few days after Father left, the wind shifted. Clouds cast shadows on the water. Whitecaps danced on the waves.

Late that night, the rain pelted the roof, and the wind howled.

Camilla came into Marcus' room. "Do you think Father is safe?" she asked.

"Yes," said Marcus. "He had clear skies on his way to Africa. He should be in port now. He will wait out this storm before he tries to come back. Don't worry."

But Camilla worried. Marcus worried, too.

In the morning, sheets of rain pounded the coastline. Mother closed the shutters tight. Wind rattled through the cracks. It was almost midday before the storm blew past.

As soon as the rain stopped, Marcus went outside. Worrying made him feel restless. He needed to find something to do.

Marcus decided to see if there was any work at the docks. He went down to the port, but it was quiet. There were no ships to unload.

"No one could have made it into port through that storm," said a dock worker. "You can run along. I don't think we will be needing you today."

Marcus wandered down the beach. The sky looked gray and milky. Gusts of wind sent the sea spray flying.

Marcus knew that in a storm, ships sailing close to land could get blown into the rocky shoreline. Sailors whose boats were in danger of sinking threw heavy cargo overboard. Marcus was glad to see that no broken pieces of ships were caught on the rocks near shore.

A large crate had washed up on the beach. Marcus hoped it held something valuable. He was disappointed when he opened it and found green, leafy vegetables.

Marcus looked out to sea. He saw what looked like a smooth, gray boulder in the water.

"That's funny," he whispered to himself. "I don't remember seeing a rock out there before."

Just then, Marcus heard Camilla shout. She was running toward him.

When she got to him, she said, "I've been calling for you, but you couldn't hear me." She leaned over and rested her hands on her knees. She tried to catch her breath.

"The wind must have blown your voice out to sea," said Marcus.

"Has anything interesting washed up?" Camilla asked.

"Not yet," said Marcus.

He looked out over the water. The object in the water came into view again. It was bigger than before.

"Camilla, look," he said as he pointed to the gray object in the waves. "I can't believe what I'm seeing!"

Camilla stood beside Marcus. They watched as a baby elephant bobbed onto the shore. As it came up onto the sand, it stumbled on its stiff, chunky legs. Although the elephant was a baby, it was taller than Marcus or Camilla. The elephant fell down at Marcus' and Camilla's feet.

Marcus knelt down beside the elephant and put his hand on its side.

"Is it alive?" Camilla asked.

"Yes," said Marcus. "It's just worn out. It must have been swimming for miles. The poor little thing needs food and water."

"I'll get water!" Camilla said. She dashed down the beach as fast as she could.

Marcus crouched over the baby elephant to protect its face from the blowing sand.

Soon, Camilla returned. She carried a big jug of water.

"We have to be able to pour the water into its mouth," she said. "I brought the biggest jug with the longest neck."

"Good thinking," said Marcus.

The children eased the top of the jug into the elephant's mouth.

As soon as the elephant tasted the water, its eyes popped open. Marcus and Camilla hopped up as the elephant struggled to its feet. It wobbled a little, but it opened its mouth for more water. Marcus held the jug in place while Camilla tipped it. The elephant emptied the jug in a hurry, and then it started to cry.

"It's hungry," said Camilla.

Marcus remembered the crate of vegetables.
He tried to lead the elephant up the beach, but it
was too weak to move.

"I'll be right back," he said.

Marcus ran up the beach to where the crate stuck out of the sand. He tore it open and pulled out a big handful of greens. He took them back to the baby elephant.

Marcus and Camilla made four more trips
back up to the crate to get food for the elephant.
Once the animal was full, it took a nap.

"What will we do with it?" asked Camilla.

"We need to make a shelter," said Marcus.
"It needs to be close to fresh water. It needs to
be hidden, so the elephant will be safe."

Camilla thought for a minute. "I know just
the place," she said. "There is a little group of
trees by the creek. The elephant could stay up
there, behind the dunes. Do you think that
might work?"

"Yes," said Marcus. "If we move its food into a heap up there, we can use the crate to build a shelter."

The children got busy. They did not dare leave the little elephant alone, so they watched it while they worked. By evening, they had a safe spot ready.

"Come with us," Marcus said to the baby elephant. "Time to go home."

The elephant followed them up the beach.

Marcus, Camilla, and the baby elephant walked
up to the new shelter next to the creek. The
elephant dipped its trunk into the creek. It
sucked up water and squirted the water into its
mouth. Then the elephant ate more greens before
it lay down and closed its eyes to sleep.

"What should its name be?" Camilla asked.

"Its name is Marina, because it came out of the sea," said Marcus.

The children did not want to leave Marina alone. Marcus decided to stay while Camilla went home.

"I'll get you some food," Camilla said. "And I will bring you a cloak. What shall I tell Mother?"

Marcus gently patted Marina's fuzzy head. "Tell her I met a new friend," he said.

Camilla came back with a basket of supplies. Mother came with her.

Soon Marina woke up. She got to her feet. She leaned into Marcus' shoulder.

"Isn't she wonderful?" Marcus said, grinning from ear to ear.

"Yes, she is," said Mother.

"Can we keep her?" Camilla asked.

"Well, she will get much larger. I'm not sure where we'll keep her," said Mother. "But for now, she is yours."

Marcus slept curled up next to Marina all night. In the morning, Marina tickled Marcus' ear with her trunk. Marcus heaped up a load of vegetables. Then he opened the basket to find some food for himself. Marina reached over and dug in the basket, too. She plucked at the grapes and ate two figs.

The grapes gave Marcus an idea. He got to his feet and dangled the cluster of grapes in front of Marina.

"Follow me," he said.

Marcus gave Marina a grape. Then he trotted down the beach. He stopped and wagged the grapes again. Marina stood for a moment, and then she trotted after him. In no time at all, Marcus could not make a move without Marina moving, too.

Camilla met them on their way back to the creek.

"She is smart! She could be in Julius Caesar's parade," said Camilla. "Remember when Caesar returned from war with 40 elephants marching beside him? The elephants carried torches with their trunks. They lit his way up the steps of the Capitol!"

"Do you think you could you carry a torch?" Marcus asked Marina.

He picked up a stick and held it. Marina wrapped her trunk around it.

"To the Capitol!" exclaimed Marcus. He led Marina and Camilla to the creek.

Even though Marcus and Camilla were busy, they had not forgotten about their father. Each day, they watched for the sails of the *Rising Star*.

"He must be on his way home by now," said Camilla. "The weather has been fair."

"Yes, but a strong wind is blowing," said Marcus. "It could be a few more days before the ship gets to port."

"Are you worried?" Camilla asked.

"Not yet," said Marcus.

A few days later, clouds gathered on the horizon. They swirled and churned like smoke. Marcus gathered his cloak around him. He looked out over the water. He did not see the bright sails of the *Rising Star*. Camilla did not see them, either.

Marcus began to worry.

Marina seemed to know how Marcus felt. She curled her trunk around his wrist.

"Mother says Father has never sailed this late in the year," said Camilla.

Marcus reached up and stroked Marina's rough cheek. "If Father can outrun that storm, he will be home by dark," he said.

"Let's hope so," said Camilla.

The children spent the day playing on the beach. Marina kept them busy, running and chasing. When Marina needed a drink, they went back to the creek.

Darkness came early, as more clouds moved in. Camilla went home to get Marcus dinner.

Marcus and Marina were on the beach when Camilla came back. She carried a torch. The flame hopped and danced over the dunes. Camilla stuck it in the sand.

"Mother says I can stay with you," Camilla said as she unpacked their dinner.

"Good," said Marcus. "I don't like these nights with no stars and no moon. I feel like I'm stuck inside a crate."

"Stuck inside a crate with an elephant," said Camilla. "That would be a tight squeeze."

Marina made a barking sound, and the children laughed.

"I have an idea," said Marcus. "Let's see if Marina can carry the torch. She did pretty well with the stick."

Camilla jumped up. She pulled the torch out of the sand. She handed it to Marcus.

Marcus held the torch. At first Marina backed away. Then she stepped a little closer.

"Don't be scared, Marina," Marcus said to her softly. "I won't let it hurt you."

Marina wrapped her trunk around the base of the torch. Marcus held on to be sure it stayed steady. He gave it a little push so that Marina would hold it up high. That way, any flying sparks would drift over their heads.

The waves were small. The light from the
torch flickered. It bounced off of the rocks that
were usually hidden far out in the waves. The
children and Marina marched up and down the
beach. Marcus pretended to be Julius Caesar.

"I am the victor!" yelled Marcus.

"All hail Caesar!" yelled Camilla.

Marina waved the torch from side to side.
She took slow, stately steps. She wound her way
along the beach. The orange flame sent its fiery
glow out over the choppy sea.

VII Homecoming

It was late when the rain started. Fat drops
pelted the sand. The children ran for the shelter
of Marina's crate. Marina followed them. She
continued to hold the torch high.

Marcus took the torch and stuck it into the ground. Then he and Camilla settled down to sleep. Camilla wrapped up in the blanket that Mother had packed for them. Marcus leaned against Marina. He watched the glow of the torch flame. He thought of Father. In his dreams, he felt the deck of the *Rising Star* lurch and buck in the storm.

Marcus woke up with a start. It was dark. Marina was gone.

At first, Marcus thought Marina was getting a drink at the creek. Then he spotted a flame out on the beach.

"Camilla, look," Marcus said as he shook Camilla's shoulder.

Camilla sat up and asked, "What is it?"

"It's Marina," said Marcus. "She's pacing along the beach. She has the torch."

Marcus picked up an apple. He went out onto the beach and called Marina's name.

Overhead, the clouds were breaking apart. Rosy dawn light filled the sky.

Marina let Marcus take the torch from her. She ate the apple. Then they walked across the sand.

Marcus did not stop at the creek. He led Marina to the riverbank near the port.

The *Rising Star* was tied up at the dock.
"Wait here," said Marcus.

Marcus left Marina and ran to the dock.
Father was coming down the gangplank.

"Father!" Marcus yelled as he waved the
torch over his head.

Father leaped onto the dock.

"Marcus! It was you!" Father said.

Marcus was confused. "What do you mean?" he asked.

"The torch," said Father. "We spotted it hours ago. We thought we were lost in the storm.

Then the flame appeared! It guided us safely into port."

"It wasn't me," Marcus said. "It was Marina. She saved you."

"Who is Marina?" Father asked.

Marcus pointed. Father turned around.

Marina was coming toward him. Mother and Camilla were close behind.

Father just stared. His mouth hung open in amazement.

"I hope you didn't bring me an elephant, Father," Marcus said with a giggle. "I already have one!"

In the story, Marcus and Camilla live in Ostia, a port on the Mediterranean Sea. It was located at the mouth of the Tiber River, about 15 miles (24 kilometers) from Rome. It was a busy place, with piers, docks, and storage buildings for shipments coming from all over the Roman Empire. Goods coming in on trade ships were moved to smaller boats or wagons. The goods were then sent by channel or by road to Rome and other cities.

Carthage was a Mediterranean port in northern Africa. The voyage from Ostia to Carthage took from three to five days, depending on the wind direction. Traders sailed from late spring to early fall, staying close to land so they could see the mountains, cliffs, temples, and lighthouses that guided their way. Once winter set in, the sea was "closed." High winds and bad weather could almost guarantee a shipwreck like the one that brought Marina and her box of vegetables onto the land.

In ancient Rome, elephants played many roles. They were used in war and also for entertainment. They were used as symbols to show the strength of the Roman Empire and its leaders. Elephants were strong for carrying supplies. They were also brave in battle.

Julius Caesar lived from 100 B.C. to 44 B.C. In the story, Marcus and Camilla act out his victory parade. It took place in 46 B.C. Torch-bearing elephants lined the ruler's path. Torch-bearing elephants later showed up on Roman coins.

In the city of Rome, trained elephants put on shows in the streets. Rich Romans had private zoos. The zoos held amazing fish, birds, and other wildlife. Elephants were popular zoo pets. Roman artists put elephants in their work. Elephants can be seen in pottery, sculptures, and metal work. Elephants represented the great size of the Roman Empire. Elephants showed that the borders of the Roman Empire reached to exotic places.

On the Web

FactHound offers a safe, fun way to find Web sites related to topics in this book. All of the sites on FactHound have been researched by our staff.

1. Visit *www.facthound.com*
2. Type in this special code: 140484063X
3. Click on the FETCH IT button.

Your trusty FactHound will fetch the best sites for you!

Look for more *Read-It!* Reader Chapter Books: Historical Tales:

DATE DUE
